THOMAS COMES
TO BREAKFAST

by
The Rev. W. Awdry

with illustrations by
John T. Kenney

GROLIER

Thomas Comes to Breakfast

THOMAS the Tank Engine has worked his Branch Line for many years. "You know just where to stop, Thomas!" laughed his Driver. "You could almost manage without me!"

Thomas had become conceited. He didn't realise his Driver was joking. "Driver says I don't need him now," he told the others.

"Don't be so daft!" snorted Percy.

"I'd never go without *my* Driver," said Toby earnestly. "I'd be frightened."

"Pooh!" boasted Thomas. "I'm not scared."

"You'd never dare!"

"I would then. You'll see!"

It was dark next morning when the Firelighter came. Thomas drowsed comfortably as the warmth spread through his boiler. He woke again in daylight. Percy and Toby were still asleep. Thomas suddenly remembered. "Silly stick-in-the-muds," he chuckled. "I'll show them! Driver hasn't come yet, so here goes."

He cautiously tried first one piston, then the other. "They're moving! They're moving!" he whispered. "I'll just go out, then I'll stop and 'wheeeeesh'. That'll make them jump!"

Very, very quietly he headed for the door.

Thomas thought he was being clever; but really he was only moving because a careless cleaner had meddled with his controls. He soon found his mistake.

He tried to "wheeeeesh", but he couldn't. He tried to stop, but he couldn't. He just kept rolling along.

"The buffers will stop me," he thought hopefully, but that siding had no buffers. It just ended at the road.

Thomas' wheels left the rails and crunched the tarmac. "Horrors!" he exclaimed, and shut his eyes. He didn't dare look at what was coming next.

The Stationmaster's family were having breakfast. They were eating ham and eggs.

There was a crash – the house rocked – broken glass tinkled – plaster peppered their plates.

Thomas had collected a bush on his travels. He peered anxiously into the room through its leaves. He couldn't speak. The Stationmaster grimly strode out and shut off steam.

His wife picked up her plate. "You miserable engine," she scolded. "Just look what you've done to our breakfast! Now I shall have to cook some more." She banged the door. More plaster fell. This time, it fell on Thomas.

Thomas felt depressed. The plaster was tickly. He wanted to sneeze, but he didn't dare in case the house fell on him. Nobody came for a long time. Everyone was much too busy.

At last workmen propped up the house with strong poles. They laid rails through the garden, and Donald and Douglas, puffing hard, managed to haul Thomas back to the Yard.

His funnel was bent. Bits of fencing, the bush, and a broken window-frame festooned his front, which was badly twisted. He looked comic.

The Twins laughed and left him. He was in disgrace.

"You are a very naughty engine."

"I know, Sir. I'm sorry, Sir." Thomas' voice was muffled behind his bush.

"You must go to the Works, and have your front end mended. It will be a long job."

"Yes, Sir," faltered Thomas.

"Meanwhile," said the Fat Controller, "a Diesel Rail-car will do your work."

"A D-D-Diesel, Sir?" Thomas spluttered.

"Yes, Thomas. Diesels *always* stay in their sheds till they are wanted. Diesels *never* gallivant off to breakfast in Stationmasters' houses." The Fat Controller turned on his heel, and sternly walked away.

Daisy

THE Fat Controller stood on the platform. Percy and Toby watched him anxiously. "Here," he said, "is Daisy, the Diesel Rail-car who has come to help while Thomas is – er – indisposed."

"Please, Sir," asked Percy, "will she go, Sir, when Thomas comes back, Sir?"

"That depends," said the Fat Controller. "Meanwhile, however long she stays, I hope you will both make her welcome and comfortable."

"Yes, Sir, we'll try, Sir," said the engines.

"Good. Run along now, and show her the Shed. She will want to rest after her journey."

Daisy was hard to please. She shuddered at the Engine Shed. "This is dreadfully smelly," she announced. "I'm highly sprung, and anything smelly is bad for my swerves."

They tried the Carriage Shed. "This is better," said Daisy, "but whatever is that rubbish?"

The "rubbish" turned out to be Annie, Clarabel, and Henrietta, who were most offended.

"We won't stay to be insulted," they fumed. Percy and Toby had to take them away, and spend half the night soothing their hurt feelings.

The engines woke next morning feeling exhausted.

Daisy, on the other hand, felt bright and cheerful. "Uu-ooo! Uu-ooo!" she tooted as she came out of the Yard, and backed to the station.

"Look at me!" she purred to the waiting passengers. "I'm the latest Diesel, highly sprung and right up to date. You won't want Thomas' bumpy old Annie and Clarabel now."

The Passengers were interested. They climbed in and sat back comfortably, waiting for Daisy to start.

Every morning a van is coupled to Thomas' first train. The farmers send their milk to the station, and Thomas takes it down to the dairy.

Thomas never minds the extra load, but Daisy did. As soon as she saw that the van was to be coupled to her, she stopped purring. "Do they expect me to pull that?" she asked indignantly.

"Surely," said her Driver, "you can pull one van."

"I won't," said Daisy. "Percy can do it. He loves messing about with trucks."

She began to shudder violently.

"Nonsense," said her Driver. "Come on now, back down."

Daisy lurched backwards. She was so cross that she blew a fuse. "Told you," she said, and stopped.

The Shunter, the Guard, the Stationmaster, and her Driver all argued with her, but it was no use.

"It's Fitter's orders," she said.

"What is?"

"My Fitter's a very nice man. He is interested in my case. He comes every week, and examines me carefully. 'Daisy,' he says, 'never, never pull. You're highly sprung, and pulling is bad for your swerves.'

"So that's how it is," finished Daisy.

"Stuff and nonsense!" said the Stationmaster.

"I can't understand," said the Shunter, "whatever made the Fat Controller send us such a feeble . . ."

"F-f-f-feeble!" spluttered Daisy. "Let me . . ."

"Stop arguing," grumbled the passengers. "We're late already."

So they uncoupled the van, and Daisy purred away feeling very pleased with herself.

"That's a good story," she chuckled. "I'll do just what work I choose and no more."

But she said it to herself.

This book club edition published by Grolier 1999

Published by arrangement with Egmont Children's Books Ltd.
The story *Thomas Comes to Breakfast* first published in Great Britain 1961 a part of *The Railway Series* No. 16
Copyright © Britt Allcroft (Thomas) LLC 1961
The story *Daisy* first published in Great Britain 1961 a part of *The Railway Series* No. 16
Copyright © Britt Allcroft (Thomas) LLC 1961

Printed in the USA